A science **The Magic School Bus®**
CHAPTER BOOK

BUTTERFLY BATTLE

SCHOLASTIC INC.
New York   Toronto   London   Auckland   Sydney
Mexico City   New Delhi   Hong Kong   Buenos Aires

Written by Nancy White.

Illustrations by Hope Gangloff.

Based on *The Magic School Bus* books
written by Joanna Cole and illustrated by Bruce Degen.

The author and editor would like to thank Dr. Lawrence F. Gall
of the Peabody Museum of Natural History at Yale University
for his expert advice in reviewing this manuscript.

ISBN 0-439-42936-6

36 35 34 33   12 13 14 15 16/0

Designed by Peter Koblish

Printed in the U.S.A.

40

INTRODUCTION

Hi, my name is Phoebe. I am one of the kids in Ms. Frizzle's class.

Maybe you've heard of Ms. Frizzle. (Sometimes we just call her the Friz.) She is a terrific teacher — but a little strange. In fact, things can get really strange in her class. Science is one of Ms. Frizzle's favorite subjects, and she knows *everything* about it.

We go on lots of field trips in the Magic School Bus.

Believe me, it's not called *magic* for nothing! Once we get on board, anything can happen.

Ms. Frizzle likes to surprise us, but we can usually tell when she is planning a special field trip — we just look at what she's wearing.

One day, the Friz came into class wearing a dress that had butterfly designs all over it. She was also wearing butterfly earrings, butterfly shoes, and a necklace that looked like a butterfly. With all those butterfly wings, the Friz looked like she might take off any minute. Little did we know that we were *all* about to take off!

You'll never guess what happened that day, but one thing's for sure: The field trips in my old school weren't *anything* like this one!

CHAPTER 1

Our classroom was absolutely quiet. Everyone was just staring straight ahead and not saying a word. This is *not* how it is most of the time in Ms. Frizzle's room. We were supposed to be working on a skit for our unit on butterflies, but no one had any ideas. So we just sat there. It was awful.

Just when we thought we couldn't stand the silence anymore, Ms. Frizzle flitted into the room wearing her butterfly outfit.

"My, but it's quiet in here," she commented. "I expected to find a flutter of activity!"

"We don't have any ideas for our butterfly skit," said Wanda.

From the Desk of Ms. Frizzle

Who Put the Butter in Butterfly?

Butterflies actually have nothing to do with butter. And butterflies are not flies. But they *are* insects. Like other insects, they have:
- Three body sections — a head in front, a middle part called the *thorax*, and a back part called the *abdomen*.
- Six legs.
- A hard outer coating called an *exoskeleton*.

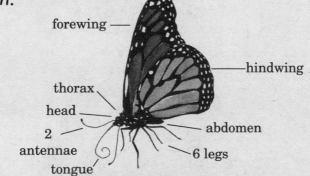

forewing

hindwing

thorax

head

abdomen

2 antennae

6 legs

tongue

Most insects also have two feelers, or *antennae*, on their heads and either two or four wings. A butterfly has two antennae and four wings.

"And the more we try, the more ideas we *don't* get," added Tim.

"I have something here that might inspire you," said Ms. Frizzle, showing us the necklace she was wearing. Hanging on a chain was a locket shaped like a butterfly, and it had the most beautiful bright and shimmery colors on its wings.

"This locket," Ms. Frizzle told us, "belonged to my great-great-grandmother Matilda. She was called Magic Matilda."

"How come they called her that?" asked Wanda. "Could she do magic tricks?"

"Great-great-grandmother Matilda was a world-famous magician," Ms. Frizzle answered proudly.

"Did Magic Matilda's locket get those beautiful colors by magic?" asked Ralphie.

"No, it didn't," answered Ms. Frizzle. "As a matter of fact, this locket is made of real butterflies' wings."

"So the locket isn't magical?" asked Arnold hopefully. Arnold, if you can believe it, is a kid who thinks a good day is when nothing special happens. His idea of fun is a couple of tests and a nice big homework assignment — *not* a magic locket.

"I don't know, Arnold," said Ms. Frizzle. "But Magic Matilda always said the locket was magical."

"I knew it," said Arnold, sounding disappointed.

"Great!" said Carlos. "Maybe it can give us an idea for our skit. Can we ask it to help us?"

"I don't think that's the kind of magic the locket has, Carlos," said Ms. Frizzle.

"What kind of magic *does* it have?" asked Tim.

"That's the wonderful mystery!" said Ms. Frizzle. "No one knows. There's a legend in my family that whoever can open the locket will possess a secret magic charm, but so far no one has been able to do it." She fiddled with the clasp on the locket as she spoke, but it didn't open.

"Excellent," said Arnold. "And with a little luck, no one ever will."

I wasn't sure I believed that the locket could really be magical, but then, strange things do happen in Ms. Frizzle's class. I decided to wait and see.

"Time to get back to our skit, class," said Ms. Frizzle, still inspecting her locket.

"What skit?" said Wanda. "We don't even have an *idea* for a skit."

"We're not even close to having an idea," said Ralphie.

"Can't you help us, Ms. Frizzle?" pleaded Keesha. "We're stuck."

Ms. Frizzle looked thoughtful. Then she grinned and said, "Well, I just might be able to help you out. What this class needs is a good field trip!"

"Here we go again," Arnold groaned. "Now we're all going to shrink down to a tiny little size and turn into butterflies. Then we'll get chased by some huge, horrible birds, or someone will catch us in a net and sell us to a natural history museum." Everyone knows that Ms. Frizzle believes in learning by doing.

"Well, you've got one thing right, Arnold," said Ms. Frizzle. "The museum has a famous butterfly collection, and I think we should go there and see it."

"As long as we're going to *see* it, and not *be* it," said Arnold. He looked like he was feeling a little better, but I couldn't help noticing that the Friz had that look in her eye. The outfit, the locket, and most of all "the look" — they all gave me the feeling that we weren't going to end up in a nice, quiet museum that day. I could tell the Friz had something much more exciting up her sleeve . . . or under her wing.

Then Ms. Frizzle said those three little words that all her students know so well: "To the bus!"

CHAPTER 2

We all piled on the bus and got in our seats. Just behind me, I heard Keesha whisper to Carlos, "I don't see how looking at butterflies in a museum is going to help us with our skit."

"Me, neither," said Carlos. "I wish we could see live butterflies instead."

I turned around and said I thought so, too. In my old school, we saw plenty of stuff in museums, but since I've been in Ms. Frizzle's class, I've gotten used to a little more excitement.

We didn't think anyone was listening, but then we noticed Liz, our class lizard, perched on the back of Keesha's seat.

She looked like she agreed with us. Later, I found out that lizards *eat* butterflies, so Liz might have had her own reasons for what she did next. She took a flying leap onto the dashboard of the bus and landed on a lever that started to flash. Then the whole bus lifted off the ground. We were flying!

"The bus is turning into a giant butterfly!" shouted Tim.

I couldn't believe it. Our bus had sprouted beautiful orange-and-black wings — two on each side. They were flapping up and down slowly and gracefully.

"What's happening, Ms. Frizzle?" I asked. I was a little scared, but excited, too.

"It seems that we've had a change in plans, class," the Friz answered cheerfully.

"I knew those plans were too good to be true," muttered Arnold.

"According to my research," said D.A., "the bus is a monarch butterfly. That means we're going south because monarchs travel to warmer climates in the fall."

D.A. was right, as usual. She knows lots of facts because she *loves* doing research. (D.A.'s real name is Dorothy Ann, but we hardly ever call her that.)

The Incredible Journey
by D.A.

Some kinds of butterflies migrate, or travel very long distances. Painted lady butterflies migrate from Africa all the way to Iceland!

What most people don't realize is that no one butterfly makes the whole round-trip migration. Butterflies don't live that long! They stop and lay eggs along the way, so new butterflies can join the flock for the rest of the trip.

Looking down, we could see the blue ocean, a beach, and then palm trees. We were over Florida! Soon the butterfly-bus landed right in front of a sign that read BUTTERFLY LAND. Behind the sign was a huge building. Well, it wasn't a building exactly. It was more like a giant tent with netting instead of solid walls or a roof. Through the netting, we could see beautiful gardens filled with brightly colored flowers.

A tour guide came running over to us. "Welcome, class. My name is Peter. I think you'll enjoy Butterfly Land just like all the other classes that come here." Peter didn't know yet that we weren't just like other classes. But he was about to find out.

"Open the door, and let's explore!" said Ms. Frizzle. We all climbed out of the bus. I couldn't wait to get a look at some live butterflies!

Before we went in, Ms. Frizzle told Liz she had to wait for us outside. "We don't want any of the butterflies to turn into lizard lunches," she said. Liz didn't mind. She eats bugs, so she thinks the whole outdoors is her snack bar.

Inside, Butterfly Land was amazing. Butterflies of all sizes and colors were flying around the trees and flowers. The first place Peter took us was the butterfly "nursery." First he showed us a plant with tiny white butterfly eggs stuck right on the leaves. They were so small, they looked like white specks.

"A female butterfly lays her eggs on a leaf," Peter told us. "She uses a sticky liquid from her body to make sure they don't fall off."

Egg ➡

Next Peter showed us baby caterpillars that had just hatched. They were tiny and had white, black, and yellow stripes.

"Someday, each caterpillar will become a butterfly," said Peter.

To: Kids
From: Peter

It's Just a Stage

Butterflies and many other insects go through four stages of life. Here is what each stage is called:

1.) **egg** – laid by a female butterfly on a leaf
2.) **larva** – the caterpillars that hatch from the eggs
3.) **pupa** – when the caterpillar grows a hard shell (sometimes called a **chrysalis**)
4.) **butterfly** – the adult stage

When an insect goes through all four stages, it's called going through complete metamorphosis. (Metamorphosis is pronounced like this: meht-uh-MOR-fuh-siss. It's a Greek word that means "a change of shape.")

"You can tell what kind of butterfly a caterpillar will become by the way it looks."

"What kind of butterfly will these caterpillars turn into?" asked Wanda.

"These will be monarch butterflies," said Peter.

"Just like our bus!" shouted Tim.

"Is that how our bus looked when it was a baby?" wondered Keesha.

Peter looked confused. Ms. Frizzle just kept smiling. "Those children have such imaginations!" she said. Peter gave us a strange look, but then he went on with his talk.

"The first thing a newborn caterpillar does," he said, "is to start eating. First it eats the shell of its own egg. Then it starts eating the leaf where it hatched. But most caterpillars will eat only a few kinds of leaves, so the butterfly has to lay her eggs on the right kind of plant. Monarchs lay their eggs only on milkweed plants."

"According to my research, milkweed is poisonous to many animals," said D.A. "And that makes the monarch caterpillar poisonous, too."

"Right you are," said Peter, looking impressed and a little surprised. I guess he'd never met a kid like D.A. before. "And it tastes terrible," he continued. "All this is good for a caterpillar because birds and other animals won't eat it. They don't like eating monarch butterflies, either."

I was wondering how the animals know that monarchs taste bad. After all, it's not like they can tell one another, "I ate one of those monarchs yesterday and it made me *really* sick." Then Peter explained, "The monarch caterpillar's colors — black and orange — are *warning colors* in nature. They tell other animals to stay away. Those warning colors are this caterpillar's defense."

"What is that thing hanging from that twig over there?" asked Wanda.

"That's a *chrysalis,*" Peter answered. "That's the form a caterpillar takes while it's getting ready to be a butterfly."

17

From Caterpillar to Chrysalis

A caterpillar grows quickly, but its skin doesn't grow at all. When the caterpillar gets too big for its skin, the skin comes off, and a new skin appears underneath. This is called molting, and it happens a few times as a caterpillar grows bigger and bigger. When a cater-

Caterpillar

Chrysalis
(pupal case)

pillar sheds its skin for the last time, there is a hard shell underneath. The caterpillar has then changed into a pupa. Chrysalis is a special name for a butterfly's pupa.

The chrysalis looked like it was made out of gold. Peter told us it would become a black-and-white butterfly called a tree nymph. The monarch chrysalis was about an inch (2.5 cm) long. It was light green with shiny gold dots and a gold stripe around the top.

"How do those wormy-looking little caterpillars get to look like beautiful gold earrings?" I asked Peter.

"Those pupas aren't moving at all," said Arnold. "Are you sure they're not dead?"

"They may not be moving on the outside," said Peter, "but inside, a lot is going on. A butterfly will come out of each of these shells!"

"What kind of butterfly will that big brown caterpillar be?" asked D.A. "The one that looks like a dead leaf."

"You can figure that out for yourself," said Peter. "I'm going to give each of you a field guide so you can look up pictures of the caterpillars and butterflies and find out what kind they are."

D.A. used her field guide right away to

look for a picture of the big brown caterpillar. "It will turn into an owl butterfly," she said. "Owl butterflies come from the rain forests of South and Central America."

Peter told us a lot more facts about butterflies. We found out that there were butterflies back in the age of the dinosaurs. We learned that the viceroy and the queen butterflies look almost exactly like the monarch but are not poisonous. Just *looking* like the monarch makes other animals leave them alone. And we learned the difference between a butterfly and a moth.

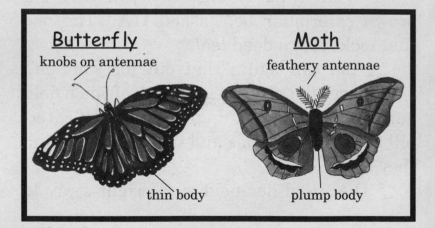

Butterfly — knobs on antennae, thin body

Moth — feathery antennae, plump body

When Peter started talking about butterflies' wings, he mentioned that some people make jewelry out of them.

Keesha called out, "Just like Magic Matilda's locket!"

We had almost forgotten about that. We were about to be reminded.

Field Guide to Butterflies

Wing Scales

A butterfly's wing is covered with tiny scales. They are something like the scales on a fish's body, but much smaller and more delicate. The scales give butterflies their beautiful colors and also help them tell one another apart. If you look at a butterfly's wing scales through a microscope, they look like this:

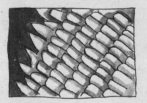 

(Different types of butterflies have differently shaped scales.)

CHAPTER 3

Ms. Frizzle lifted up her locket to show it to Peter. "It's made from the wings of a flutterby — I mean butterfly," she said, laughing at her own mistake. We all laughed, too.

At that moment, she must have accidentally pressed a secret catch or something, because the locket opened! We froze, waiting to see what would happen. At first, nothing did.

"I knew that locket wasn't really magic," said Ralphie. He walked away to look at a beautiful shiny butterfly called a blue morpho.

"Isn't this interesting, class?" said Ms. Frizzle. (She thinks *everything* is interesting.) "There's some pink powder inside the locket."

Now we gathered around and held our breath with excitement. Arnold was standing right next to the Friz. He looked like he was about to explode, and when he couldn't hold his breath any longer, he breathed out really hard. When he did that, he blew the pink powder out of the locket and all over us — some of it even got on Ms. Frizzle!

Luckily, none got on Peter, who had turned to look at the blue morpho. When Peter turned around again, all he saw was our field guides in a pile on the ground — and Ms. Frizzle's locket lying on top. He kept looking around and saying to himself, "Where did they go? Where did they go?"

But we hadn't gone anywhere. We had turned into butterflies!

"Isn't this wonderful, class?" said Butterfly-Friz. Ms. Frizzle always gets very excited when we turn into something. "Now our field trip is *really* taking off!"

At first, I was afraid I wouldn't know how to fly, but when I saw all the other kid-butterflies — even Arnold — flying around

from flower to flower, I decided to join in the fun. And there was a lot of it. Just imagine flitting around a garden all day and drinking sweet, delicious nectar from flowers whenever you get hungry!

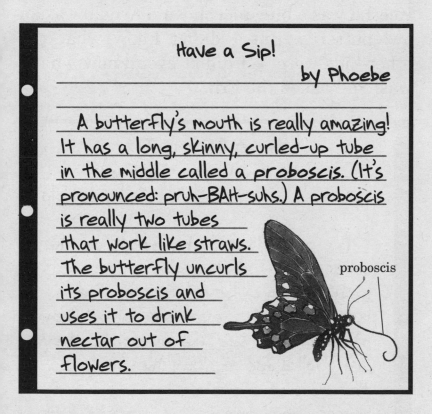

Have a Sip!
by Phoebe

A butterfly's mouth is really amazing! It has a long, skinny, curled-up tube in the middle called a proboscis. (It's pronounced: pruh-BAH-suhs.) A proboscis is really two tubes that work like straws. The butterfly uncurls its proboscis and uses it to drink nectar out of flowers.

proboscis

Each of us was a different kind of butterfly. That probably wouldn't happen in nature, because the same kinds of butterflies usually stay together around the same kinds of plants. But here in Butterfly Land, all kinds of butterflies could hang out together.

From our tour with Peter, I knew that Keesha was a blue morpho and Arnold was an owl butterfly. But I didn't know what the other kids were — I didn't even know what *I* was! So I asked the Friz.

The Owl Butterfly
(It's Giving You the Eye)
by Arnold

The owl butterfly has spots on the undersides of its rear wings. The spots look like big owl eyes. Some other butterflies have "eyespots," also. When other animals see the eyespots, they are fooled into thinking they're the eyes of a much bigger animal, and they get scared. So eyespots are a kind of butterfly defense.

Owl

She looked around and said, "Well, let's see. If I remember my butterflies correctly, Carlos is a tiger swallowtail, Wanda is a painted lady, Tim is a red admiral, D.A. is a zebra longwing, and you, Phoebe, are a monarch."

"What are you, Ms. Frizzle?" I asked.

"Good question, Phoebe," she said. "Tell me what I look like."

"Well, your wings are mostly brownish-orange with a black stripe and little white dots around the edge," I told her. "You look sort of like a monarch, but not as brightly colored."

"It sounds like I'm a queen butterfly, Phoebe," she said. Then she flew away.

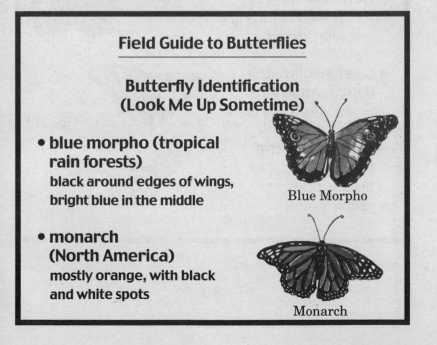

Field Guide to Butterflies

Butterfly Identification (Look Me Up Sometime)

- **blue morpho (tropical rain forests)**
  black around edges of wings, bright blue in the middle

  Blue Morpho

- **monarch (North America)**
  mostly orange, with black and white spots

  Monarch

- **owl (tropical rain forests)**
  mostly brown, with purple in the middle of its eyespots

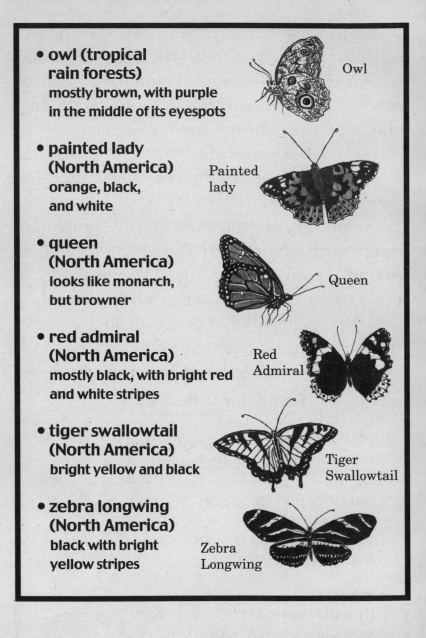

Owl

- **painted lady (North America)**
  orange, black, and white

Painted lady

- **queen (North America)**
  looks like monarch, but browner

Queen

- **red admiral (North America)**
  mostly black, with bright red and white stripes

Red Admiral

- **tiger swallowtail (North America)**
  bright yellow and black

Tiger Swallowtail

- **zebra longwing (North America)**
  black with bright yellow stripes

Zebra Longwing

I started to follow Ms. Frizzle, but all of a sudden, something seemed wrong. When I tried to remember what kind of butterfly each kid was, I only counted seven kinds. And there should have been eight of us. Someone was missing. Ralphie!

"Ralphie! Where are you, Ralphie?" I yelled. But no one answered. When the other kids heard me, they all started calling Ralphie's name, too, and so did Ms. Frizzle. But no Ralphie.

"Where could he be?" asked Tim.

"Hey, I have an idea," said Wanda. "Remember when Arnold blew the pink powder out of Magic Matilda's locket?"

"You don't have to rub it in," said Arnold.

"Well, you did, Arnold," said Wanda. Then she went on. "Ralphie wasn't with the group. He was over with Peter looking at the blue morpho."

"So you mean Ralphie didn't get any pink powder on him?" asked Carlos. "But then he'd still be a regular kid, and we'd be able to see him."

"Or — maybe he just got a *little* on him," said Keesha. "Not enough to turn him into a butterfly, but just enough to . . ."

". . . turn him into a caterpillar!" we all yelled out together.

"I love it when those butterfly brains go to work!" said Ms. Frizzle. "Come on, class. Let's see if we can find Ralphie on one of these leaves."

There were so many plants in Butterfly Land, I wondered how we would ever find Ralphie.

Then I heard Tim shouting, "There he is! That's him!"

"How can you tell it's really Ralphie?" asked Carlos.

"A caterpillar wearing a red baseball cap?" said Tim. "Who else could it be?"

I spotted Ralphie. He was a prickly, spiny-looking black caterpillar with lots of legs. He had rows of orange spots along his back and sides. He had blue dots, too. And he was wearing his red baseball cap.

Creeping Caterpillars
by Ralphie

Caterpillars look like worms, but they're not. A caterpillar is the larva stage of a butterfly.

A caterpillar's head has two short feelers. Its mouth is different from a butterfly's because it's made for chewing leaves, not sipping nectar.

A caterpillar's body has six front legs. They will be the butterfly's legs. It also has as many as 10 legs in back. Those are called prolegs, and they disappear when the caterpillar molts for the last time. A caterpillar has tiny holes in the sides of its body. They're for breathing. They're called spiracles. (Butterflies and other insects get air through spiracles, too.)

Ralphie was on the green leaf of a plant with yellow flowers. The leaf was near the ground, near the entrance to Butterfly Land. But before we could say anything, Ralphie, red baseball cap and all, crawled through an opening under the door and was gone!

CHAPTER 2

"We have to find Ralphie. We just have to!" said D.A. "According to my research, it's very dangerous for him out there. Most caterpillars don't even live long enough to become butterflies." Then she started listing all the animals that eat caterpillars. "Birds, moles, mice, ants, toads, wasps, spiders —"

"Okay, okay, we get the idea, D.A.," said Tim. "There are lots of predators out there that might think Ralphie is a tasty snack. We have to figure out how to find him before . . . before . . . well, before you-know-what."

I knew D.A. and Tim were right. We had

to get Ralphie back to Butterfly Land, where he would be safe.

"The first thing we have to figure out," said Wanda, "is how to get out of Butterfly Land. We're too big to fit under the door the way Ralphie did."

I looked outside, wondering how to get out there. That's when I spotted Liz. "Hey, you guys," I called to the other kids. "Maybe Liz can help us get out."

"She did get us *into* this mess in the first place," said Arnold, remembering how Liz had made the bus turn into a butterfly.

I didn't want to say anything, but Arnold sort of *blew* it, too!

Just saying Liz's name got her attention. "Get us out of here, Liz," Carlos called to her.

Just then, a whole class of kids that had been lined up outside came in through the entrance door. After the last kid was inside, Liz held the door open just long enough for us to fly out without anyone noticing. Now we could start looking for a caterpillar wearing a red baseball cap. But first, we needed to come up with a plan. We settled on a big rock that was warm from the sun to figure things out.

"This feels so-o-o-o good," said Wanda.

"I feel like I'm getting more energy," said Tim. "I was feeling kind of tired before."

A Place in the Sun
by Wanda

Butterflies can't fly unless their body temperature is very warm, like the temperature on a nice summer day. Since butterflies are cold-blooded, their body temperature goes down when the temperature outside goes down. They bask in the sun to get their body temperatures up again.

Lizards are cold-blooded, too. They bask in the sun for the same reason.

Now I could see why Liz's favorite place to sit was on a rock in the sun.

After we sunbathed, we folded our wings straight up over our bodies. Anyone walking by would hardly have noticed us there, because most butterflies' wings are not brightly colored on the bottom — only on the top. And it's the bottom part that shows when their wings are folded together. Most of us blended right in with the rock.

"Uh-oh, birds," said Tim. We could hear them twittering in the bushes nearby. "Don't they eat butterflies?"

We had all been so worried about what could happen to a caterpillar outside the safety of Butterfly Land, we had forgotten one important thing. Lots of predators like butterflies, too. We had more than birds to worry about. Bats, wasps, and, of course, lizards like to eat butterflies. When we were human kids, we were on top of the food chain. Now we were a lot closer to the bottom, which was pretty scary. You can take it from someone who's been there!

The Food Chain Is No Diamond Necklace

by Arnold

Plants get eaten, but they don't eat, so they're at the bottom of the food chain. The animals that are lowest on the food chain eat mainly plants, but they get eaten by lots of other animals. It's a food-eat-food world out there, but the higher you are on the food chain, the less likely you are to get eaten. Big meat eaters like lions and wolves are up pretty high. Humans are at the top. Butterflies are a lot further down.

Since only some of the kids had wings that blended into the background, Ms. Frizzle had them surround the ones who still stood out — like me! Fortunately, the birds didn't bother us. Ms. Frizzle — or you could say Madame Butterfly — told us why. "You're *cam-*

ouflaged. Camouflage is when an animal blends in with its background so predators don't notice it. Life is splendid when you're blended!"

Then Arnold had a good idea. "Peter said that most caterpillars only like to eat a few special kinds of leaves. The leaf Ralphie was on was part of a plant with yellow flowers. If we can find plants like that, maybe we can find Ralphie."

"Rightly reasoned, Arnold!" said Butterfly-Friz. "And for your information, the name of that plant is toadflax."

So we flew off to look for toadflax plants, and soon we found some. Ralphie wasn't there, but someone else was. On a tree above us was a whole flock of birds. This time our wings were spread out, so we weren't camouflaged. Before I could say, "Butterflies, flutter by!" the birds were swooping down on us. I couldn't figure out why they weren't chasing Ms. Frizzle or me, and then I remembered I was a monarch — the kind of butterfly birds don't like to eat. And the Friz was a queen — one of the butterflies that looks like a monarch. But Arnold was in big trouble.

"Hey, Arnold, look out!" I yelled.

A really big bird was coming right at Arnold. Its huge wings were flapping and its pointed beak was wide open.

"Help!" screamed Arnold. "Somebody do something!"

But we couldn't do anything to save him. The big bird was getting closer and closer. I covered my eyes so I wouldn't see Arnold get turned into bird food.

My heart was pounding when I heard Keesha yell out, "Flash your eyespots!"

I peeked through my fingers just in time to see Arnold flip up his wings and show his eyespots. Lucky for him he was an owl butterfly! Those eyespots on his wings scared the bird away. It must have thought that it was looking into the eyes of a big fierce owl instead of at the wings of a harmless little butterfly. I breathed a sigh of relief. Arnold had just barely escaped.

"Well done, Arnold," said Ms. Frizzle. "Now *that's* what I call learning by doing!"

♥CHAPTER 5♥

We rested in the sun for a while to get our energy back. Then Tim flew up in the air. "Let's get going!" he called down to the rest of us.

"Ralphie, get ready to be rescued!" chimed in Wanda.

"Can't we have a quick lunch first?" said Carlos. "I'm starved."

"Yeah, a nice juicy burger sounds good," said Arnold. "With lots of fries."

"We butterflies need flower power, Arnold. The kind of food we eat comes from flowers," said Ms. Frizzle. "I'm dreaming of some milkweed nectar."

"Now that you mention it, I'd love some daisies," said Wanda.

"And what I wouldn't do for some honeysuckle," Carlos chimed in.

"Picky, picky," said Keesha.

"That's how we butterflies are," said D.A. "I, myself, will be looking for passionflowers."

"I say we look for a garden," said Keesha. "That way we can all find something we want to eat."

So off we went in search of a garden. We must have taken a wrong turn somewhere, though, because we were suddenly flying over a city! Everywhere we looked, there were huge buildings in our way. We couldn't see any grass, and there were only a few trees. There wasn't a flower in sight!

"Birds aren't the only danger for butterflies," said Ms. Frizzle. "When buildings and parking lots go up, they don't leave much room for fields and gardens. A butterfly can get mighty hungry!"

"I don't think I can go on any longer," said Carlos after a while.

"Me, neither," said Keesha. Her wings were drooping, and she looked like she was fluttering in slow motion.

All of us were feeling so weak and hungry, we were about ready to drop.

"Don't give up!" said Ms. Frizzle. "When the going gets tough, the tough keep fluttering."

"Who said butterflies were tough?" asked Arnold.

"They're tougher than you think," said the Friz. "Remember what Peter said — butterflies have survived for millions of years. Dinosaurs have been extinct for a long time, but we butterflies are still around."

That didn't really make us feel much better, but when she said, "Think of Ralphie!" we knew we couldn't give up.

"Look down there!" shouted Carlos. "Flowers!"

Carlos was right. We were flying over a park. We all landed and headed straight for the kinds of flowers we needed. Somehow, no one had to tell us — we all just knew where to go. But before anyone had a bite — or should I say a sip — Ms. Frizzle yelled, "Stop! Don't touch another thing in this park. Let's get out of here fast!"

As tired and hungry as we were, we followed the Friz.

"What happened, Ms. Frizzle? Why can't we feed from the flowers?" Keesha asked.

"Look at that truck down there," Ms. Frizzle answered. "See how it's spraying stuff

all over the park? That's insecticide." She told us that insecticide is a mixture of chemicals used to kill insects so they won't bother people or destroy plants.

"And we're insects, right?" asked Tim.

"Yes, I'm afraid we are," said the Friz. "We're lucky we got out of there alive."

"Look!" Wanda cried, after we'd flown only a little farther. "Now *that* is the biggest garden I've ever seen."

"Let's go check it out. Maybe we'll get some lunch after all," said Tim.

As we got closer to the huge garden Wanda had spotted, we saw a sign that read, CITY BOTANICAL GARDEN AND WILDLIFE PRESERVE.

We were really in luck. The garden was big and beautiful, with almost every kind of flower you can imagine. And a special part of the garden was called the Butterfly Garden. The flowers there had been planted especially to attract all kinds of butterflies so that people could enjoy looking at them.

What's the Sense?

by Wanda

Butterflies can see, taste, feel, smell, and hear.

See: A butterfly's eye is really lots of little eyes, so a butterfly sees many small pictures of the same thing instead of just one picture, like we do. Caterpillars can hardly see at all.

Taste: Butterflies taste mainly with their feet! The proboscis can taste, too.

Feel: Butterflies feel with tiny hairs all over their bodies and on their antennae.

Smell: Butterflies smell with their antennae, legs, and other parts of their bodies.

Hear: Some butterflies don't have ears, and some hear sounds through their body.

"Have a lovely lunch, class," said Ms. Frizzle, heading straight for the milkweed. In my old school, we had milk for lunch — not milkweed. But I followed right behind her, anyway.

Soon we felt like ourselves again. Well, not exactly like ourselves. After all, we were still butterflies. But before long, the Ralphie Rescue Squad was off and flying again.

CHAPTER 6

It didn't take us long to find Ralphie. There was plenty of toadflax at the botanical garden, and the red baseball cap made Ralphie stand out. None of the other caterpillars was wearing a hat.

We settled on the flowers and called out, "Hey, Ralphie, it's us!"

"It's about time," said Ralphie. "I thought I was one cooked caterpillar."

"What happened?" said Keesha.

"As soon as I left Butterfly Land, a bird swooped down and picked me up in its beak. I was just lucky that I got dropped here instead of swallowed."

"So you might say you got here by air-mail," said Carlos.

"The problem is," said D.A., "we have to get back to the safety of Butterfly Land before something really terrible happens."

"But how are we going to get Ralphie back?" asked Tim. "He can't fly, and he's too heavy to carry. Besides, if we tried, we might squash him."

Ms. Frizzle always says that if you think hard enough about a problem, you'll come up with a solution. So I made a suggestion. "Let's go over what we've learned about caterpillars and butterflies. Maybe we'll come up with an idea," I said. "Everyone say one thing we've learned."

"Butterflies are insects," said Arnold.

"We know the difference between a moth and a butterfly," said Wanda.

"We know that caterpillars turn into butterflies," said Keesha.

"Bingo!" said Carlos. "That's it! Ralphie isn't a butterfly *yet,* but he will be."

D.A. said, "According to my research,

that could take a very long time. Ralphie could spend weeks as a caterpillar and more weeks as a chrysalis."

"That's true," said Keesha, "but maybe the little bit of pink powder that got on Ralphie could make this all go faster than usual."

"How many times have you molted so far, Ralphie?" asked Wanda.

Right on Time: Butterfly Timetable
by D.A.

It can take from three days up to a whole winter for a caterpillar to hatch from an egg.

The caterpillar stage can last from one month up to three years.

The chrysalis stage can take one week, a few months, or even a dozen years!

Most butterflies only live from two to four weeks, but some live longer.

"Three, if I remember correctly," Ralphie answered. "And now that you mention it, my skin feels kind of tight right now. I think I'm ready to molt again."

That was good news, because it meant that soon Ralphie would become a chrysalis like the ones Peter showed us at Butterfly Land. And that meant he'd be one step closer to being a butterfly. Keesha was right. The pink powder had put Ralphie on fast-forward.

Just then, things got really strange. Ralphie started looking nervous. He crawled off his leaf and into a pile of dead branches. The next thing we knew, he was hanging upside down from a twig! He had spun a little pad of silk on the twig and was holding on to it with his two rear legs. Soon he started wiggling around like crazy. Then his skin split right in two just behind his head!

"Ouch! That must really hurt," said Arnold. But Ms. Frizzle told us that it didn't hurt Ralphie at all. He had to get out of that old skin so he could start turning into a butterfly.

Sure enough, the skin split some more

and started to come off. Finally, it was all dried and bunched up right where Ralphie's abdomen was attached to the twig.

The Ralphie that came out of the skin looked completely different — not like his old caterpillar self at all. Now he was a chrysalis. He had no legs or spine, and no orange or blue spots. He was a brownish-grayish color.

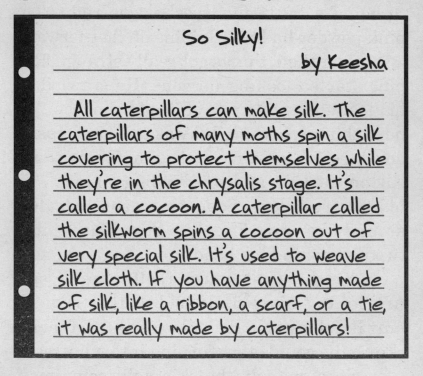

So Silky!

by Keesha

All caterpillars can make silk. The caterpillars of many moths spin a silk covering to protect themselves while they're in the chrysalis stage. It's called a cocoon. A caterpillar called the silkworm spins a cocoon out of very special silk. It's used to weave silk cloth. If you have anything made of silk, like a ribbon, a scarf, or a tie, it was really made by caterpillars!

Next, Ralphie did something amazing. He twisted and turned until his body was completely free of the old skin. To do that, he had to let go of his silk pad for a second, hold on to the old skin that was still stuck to the twig, and then reattach himself to the twig next to the old skin.

"Nice gymnastics, Ralphie!" Keesha called out. But Ralphie wasn't listening. He just hung there in his brown shell, which was getting hard and dry.

"Is he . . . ?" Arnold started to ask. Arnold was afraid Ralphie was dead, but when I reminded him of what we'd learned at Butterfly Land, he felt better. Still, it was weird to see Ralphie just hanging there.

After a while, the old skin dried up and fell to the ground. Inside his shell, we knew that Ralphie's body was slowly changing. He was growing wings and everything he would need to be a butterfly.

Now there was nothing left for us to do but wait.

From Caterpillar to Chrysalis
(You've Changed!)

These pictures show how a caterpillar becomes a chrysalis.

The caterpillar hangs upside down from its silk pad.

Its skin splits near the head.

Its skin comes off the caterpillar's body.

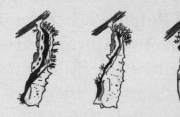

The caterpillar gets rid of old skin. Underneath is a hard shell.

The caterpillar becomes a chrysalis.

CHAPTER 7

"According to my research," said D.A., "the chrysalis will split open near Ralphie's head, and Butterfly-Ralphie will come out."

"I hope it happens soon," said Arnold. "The sooner that chrysalis splits, the sooner *we* can split — out of here and back to Butterfly Land. At least they don't allow birds in there."

We waited, and waited, and waited . . . and then it happened. The chrysalis split open. Tim got so excited, he started describing what was happening as if he were a sports announcer.

"The opening in the chrysalis is getting bigger. And what do we see? It's round and black. Is it a . . . ? Yes, it is! It's a head, folks — a round black head, and it's wearing a red baseball cap. And now Ralphie is pushing with all his strength. Can he do it? Can he get his whole body out of the chrysalis?"

"Come on, Ralphie!" we all shouted, cheering him on.

Then Tim started announcing again. "What's coming out next, folks? It's the antennae. And now for the wings. They're coming out. They're out! And Ralphie is free of the chrysalis. But wait a minute." Tim sounded worried. "Look at those wings! They're hanging down all wet and crumpled up. Is something wrong? Let's ask Ms. Frizzle." Tim pretended he was holding a microphone up to the Friz. He was really getting into this announcer thing.

"Nothing's wrong," said Ms. Frizzle. "A butterfly's wings have to be crumpled up like that or they would never fit inside the chrysalis. Soon Ralphie will pump a liquid from his body into the veins in his wings. That will make the wings stretch out straight. Then they will dry out."

"Thank you, Ms. Frizzle," said Tim, still using his loud fake-announcer voice. "She's right, folks. Those wings are starting to straighten out right now. And look at this — Ralphie is taking his first steps as a butterfly."

"Way to go, Ralphie!" we all cheered as Butterfly-Ralphie took his first steps along the twig he had been hanging from.

Soon Ralphie's wings dried out, just like Ms. Frizzle said they would. But the first time he tried to fly, he fell back down in the grass.

"Don't worry," Ms. Frizzle told us. "Ralphie's new at this, but he'll learn. Let him try, and then he'll fly!"

Ralphie climbed up the stem of a large flower and rested on top of the flower for a few minutes.

"Are you getting energy from the sun, Ralphie?" Wanda asked him.

Ralphie was still too weak to answer.

Then Tim the announcer took over again. "He's started moving his wings up and down, folks. And there he goes — up, up, up into the wild blue yonder! Fly, Ralphie, fly!"

"It's a bird, it's a plane, it's Ralphie!" yelled Carlos.

"Wow, that was awesome," said Ralphie. Then he asked, "Hey, how do I look? What kind of butterfly am I?"

"You're mostly brown, with orange stripes and eyespots on all four of your wings," I told him. "You look very nice."

I remembered a butterfly just like Ralphie from my field guide. I told him I thought he was a buckeye.

Field Guide to Butterflies

The Buckeye Butterfly

The buckeye can be found throughout most of the United States in fields and meadows in the summertime. The buckeye caterpillar feeds on plantain, toadflax, and gerardia. In butterfly form, buckeyes like to bask on bare ground and visit mud puddles.

"Now that we're all butterflies," said Arnold, "let's get back to Butterfly Land — before we're all toast!"

"Is everyone ready?" asked Ms. Frizzle. "Let's count down."

We all counted down from ten together: "Ten, nine, eight, seven, six, five, four, three, two, one . . . flutter!" We took off into the air — Butterfly-Friz and all eight of us butterfly kids, together at last.

But getting back to Butterfly Land wasn't as easy as we thought it would be. Suddenly, instead of fluttering along, we were swirling and tumbling around in the air, completely out of control.

"What's going on?" shouted Wanda.

"I feel like I'm on a roller coaster!" yelled Ralphie. "But I'm not having any fun!"

I didn't know what had hit us, but I agreed with Ralphie. This was no fun at all.

Then I heard Keesha's voice as she swept past me. "It's the wind," she called out. "Really strong winnnnn . . ." Her voice trailed off so I couldn't hear her anymore, but I saw her go whirling out of sight.

I tried to follow Keesha, but it was no use. A strong gust of wind had swept us up and was tossing us around in the air like dry leaves in a hurricane. I was feeling kind of seasick — airsick, I guess — when the wind finally died down. I settled on the branch of a tree and waited for the others. The first to land next to me was the Friz.

"That was a scary experience, Ms. Frizzle," I said.

"A *learning* experience, Phoebe," she corrected me. "Now we know how dangerous wind can be for butterflies. I've heard that one hurricane can temporarily wipe out the whole butterfly population on a small tropical island!"

"Um, that's very interesting," I said, still feeling a little sick. I didn't want to hurt the Friz's feelings, but I was glad that the learning experience was over.

The Friz actually looked like she was

enjoying herself. Sometimes she gets a little carried away. This time we *all* got carried away — for real!

We waited until the rest of the kids joined us, then we took off again, looking for somewhere we could rest.

The wind had carried us off course, so we had to land in a park. It looked safe — little did we know what was in store for us. We'd battled birds, buildings, insecticides, and wind — and now we were about to fight the biggest battle of our butterfly lives!

CHAPTER 8

We settled on some flowers in the park, but we weren't taking any more chances with insecticide, so we didn't feed.

As we rested up from our windy adventure, a group of noisy kids came running into the park. At first, we didn't worry about them. After all, they were just kids — like us. Only they weren't just like us — because we were butterflies.

"What are they carrying?" Wanda asked.

"Some kind of nets," said Tim. "Maybe they're going fishing."

"I don't see any lake or pond around here," said Keesha.

"And they don't have fishing poles," said Carlos.

"Um . . . I think they're butterfly nets," said Wanda.

That's when we noticed that the kids were carrying jars, too. They were the size of mayonnaise jars — just big enough to hold a butterfly.

"Oh, no," Arnold groaned. "Not another adventure."

We stayed very still with our wings folded, hoping the kids wouldn't notice us. They had quieted down now and were tiptoe-ing around the park, hoping to sneak up on some helpless butterflies like us. We could hear some of them whispering to one another.

"They're so pretty," said one girl.

"I know. I hope we catch a lot," her friend answered.

That freaked Arnold out. He got so scared, he started to fly. Then . . . *WOMP!* A net came down over him and trapped him on the grass.

"I got one," yelled one of the boys.

Too bad Arnold's owl butterfly eyespots

weren't going to fool a human the way they fooled a bird. The next moment, Arnold was in a jar with a lid full of holes.

"Let's see if we can find some more," one of the other kids called out.

Just when it looked like we'd lose the butterfly battle for sure, a woman in a uniform rode into the park on a horse. She was a park ranger.

"Hi, kids," she said in a friendly voice. "What are you up to with those nets?"

"We're catching butterflies," said one of the girls.

"Sorry," said the ranger, "but that's not allowed here. We protect the butterflies in this park so that everyone can enjoy their beauty."

As soon as the ranger said that, the boy held up his jar with Arnold in it. "I caught one already," he said. "But I didn't hurt it."

"That's good," said the ranger. "Thank you for telling me. Why don't you let it go now?"

The boy opened the jar, and Arnold flew out.

"Let's get out of here," Arnold said as soon as he was out of his jar.

"Up, up, and away, class!" said Ms. Frizzle.

We flew as fast as we could, and soon we reached Butterfly Land. It was good to be back, but we still had two big problems.

Big problem number one: How would we get back inside?

Big problem number two: How would we ever get to be kids again?

And to think that just this morning, the only problem we had was coming up with an idea for our skit!

CHAPTER 9

"Where's Liz?" asked Carlos. "She got us out of Butterfly Land. Maybe she can get us back in."

We looked around for Liz, but we didn't see her anywhere. But we did see our bus parked outside. The lights were flashing on and off.

"I think the bus is signaling us," said Wanda.

As we got closer to the bus, we saw that the door was open and Liz was at the controls. On the floor next to her were our field guides piled up in a neat stack. And on top of the stack was Ms. Frizzle's great-great-grandmother Matilda's locket. Peter must have put those things there. Or maybe Liz . . . It didn't seem possible, but you never know.

"If only we could open Magic Matilda's locket," said Keesha. "It turned us into butterflies. Maybe it could turn us back into kids."

"How *did* you open the locket, Ms. Frizzle?" I asked.

"I don't know, Phoebe," said the Friz. "But

if we all think very hard, I'm sure we'll come up with the answer. Turn on those butterfly brains!"

"All I remember," said Carlos, "is that Peter was talking about butterfly jewelry."

"And I mentioned Ms. Frizzle's locket," said Keesha.

"Then Ms. Frizzle asked Peter if he wanted to see it, and she lifted it up to show him," Tim remembered.

"And then it just opened," said Wanda.

That gave me an idea. "Wait a minute," I said. "Ms. Frizzle said something before the locket opened. I remember, because we all laughed."

"That's right!" said D.A. "Do you remember what you said, Ms. Frizzle? Maybe those were magic words that opened the locket."

"I think I meant to say the word *butterfly,* but by mistake I said *flutterby.*"

As soon as she said it, the locket snapped opened. It was filled with powder again, but this time the powder was green.

"I'll bet that powder will turn us back into kids," said Ralphie.

We fluttered around the open locket and

beat our wings up and down as hard as we could to blow the powder out. It worked! Before we knew it, we were our old selves. Our butterfly battle had been exciting, but I have to admit I was glad to be a kid again.

Ms. Frizzle was back in the driver's seat. Liz pushed some buttons and turned some knobs, and our bus turned back into a butterfly. I was glad it was the bus — and not us! We waved good-bye to Butterfly Land and finally headed for home.

When we got back to school, everything was the same except for one very important thing. Now we had plenty of ideas for our skit!

"We can just act out what happened on our field trip," said Ralphie.

"No one will believe it, but they'll like it, anyway," said Tim.

"Ms. Frizzle, can we use your locket for our skit?" I asked.

The Friz smiled as she handed us some string and some modeling clay. "Maybe it would be better if you made a pretend locket for the skit," she said.

A Letter from Ms. Frizzle

Planting a Butterfly Garden

Dear Readers,

    Because there are now so many cities and suburbs where there used to be farmland, fields, and marshes, many butterflies are losing their homes. To help save these beautiful insects, you can plant a special garden for butterflies.

    Your first step is to do some research. Find out what kinds of butterflies live around your area. Then find out which kinds of plants those butterflies are attracted to when they are caterpillars. A good field guide to butterflies will give you the information you need.

    After you've done your research, your next step is to choose a spot for your garden. It should get plenty of sun and not too much wind.

    At the plant store, you can buy

either seeds or *seedlings* — tiny baby plants that have already started to grow. Try planting patches of the same flower instead of just one or two plants in one spot. Oh, yes, and one more very important thing — no insecticides!

To help you get started, here are some flowers that are easy to grow.

Clover	Lantana
Milkweed	Aster
Dogbane	Vetch
Thistle	Joe-pye weed

These flowers will attract many butterflies to your beautiful garden. You can begin with just three or four kinds.

Have fun, and good luck with your butterfly garden!

Ms. Frizzle

P.S. If you look in your garden one day and see a caterpillar wearing a red baseball cap, please let me know!